A Simple S

Gustave Flaubert

Alpha Editions

This edition published in 2023

ISBN : 9789357935920

Design and Setting By
Alpha Editions
www.alphaedis.com
Email - info@alphaedis.com

Contents

CHAPTER I

For half a century the housewives of Pont-l'Eveque had envied Madame Aubain her servant Felicite.

For a hundred francs a year, she cooked and did the housework, washed, ironed, mended, harnessed the horse, fattened the poultry, made the butter and remained faithful to her mistress—although the latter was by no means an agreeable person.

Madame Aubain had married a comely youth without any money, who died in the beginning of 1809, leaving her with two young children and a number of debts. She sold all her property excepting the farm of Toucques and the farm of Geffosses, the income of which barely amounted to 5,000 francs; then she left her house in Saint-Melaine, and moved into a less pretentious one which had belonged to her ancestors and stood back of the market-place. This house, with its slate-covered roof, was built between a passage-way and a narrow street that led to the river. The interior was so unevenly graded that it caused people to stumble. A narrow hall separated the kitchen from the parlour, where Madame Aubain sat all day in a straw armchair near the window. Eight mahogany chairs stood in a row against the white wainscoting. An old piano, standing beneath a barometer, was covered with a pyramid of old books and boxes. On either side of the yellow marble mantelpiece, in Louis XV. style, stood a tapestry armchair. The clock represented a temple of Vesta; and the whole room smelled musty, as it was on a lower level than the garden.

On the first floor was Madame's bed-chamber, a large room papered in a flowered design and containing the portrait of Monsieur dressed in the costume of a dandy. It communicated with a smaller room, in which there were two little cribs, without any mattresses. Next, came the parlour (always closed), filled with furniture covered with sheets. Then a hall, which led to the study, where books and papers were piled on the shelves of a book-case that enclosed three quarters of the big black desk. Two panels were entirely hidden under pen-and-ink sketches, Gouache landscapes and Audran engravings, relics of better times and vanished luxury. On the second floor, a garret-window lighted Felicite's room, which looked out upon the meadows.

She arose at daybreak, in order to attend mass, and she worked without interruption until night; then, when dinner was over, the dishes cleared away and the door securely locked, she would bury the log under the ashes and fall asleep in front of the hearth with a rosary in her hand. Nobody could bargain with greater obstinacy, and as for cleanliness, the lustre on her brass sauce-pans was the envy and despair of other servants. She was most economical, and when she ate she would gather up crumbs with the tip of her finger, so that nothing should be wasted of the loaf of bread weighing twelve pounds which was baked especially for her and lasted three weeks.

Summer and winter she wore a dimity kerchief fastened in the back with a pin, a cap which concealed her hair, a red skirt, grey stockings, and an apron with a bib like those worn by hospital nurses.

Her face was thin and her voice shrill. When she was twenty-five, she looked forty. After she had passed fifty, nobody could tell her age; erect and silent always, she resembled a wooden figure working automatically.

CHAPTER II

Like every other woman, she had had an affair of the heart. Her father, who was a mason, was killed by falling from a scaffolding. Then her mother died and her sisters went their different ways; a farmer took her in, and while she was quite small, let her keep cows in the fields. She was clad in miserable rags, beaten for the slightest offence and finally dismissed for a theft of thirty sous which she did not commit. She took service on another farm where she tended the poultry; and as she was well thought of by her master, her fellow-workers soon grew jealous.

One evening in August (she was then eighteen years old), they persuaded her to accompany them to the fair at Colleville. She was immediately dazzled by the noise, the lights in the trees, the brightness of the dresses, the laces and gold crosses, and the crowd of people all hopping at the same time. She was standing modestly at a distance, when presently a young man of well-to-do appearance, who had been leaning on the pole of a wagon and smoking his pipe, approached her, and asked her for a dance. He treated her to cider and cake, bought her a silk shawl, and then, thinking she had guessed his purpose, offered to see her home. When they came to the end of a field he threw her down brutally. But she grew frightened and screamed, and he walked off.

One evening, on the road leading to Beaumont, she came upon a wagon loaded with hay, and when she overtook it, she recognised Theodore. He greeted her calmly, and asked her to forget what had happened between them, as it "was all the fault of the drink."

She did not know what to reply and wished to run away.

Presently he began to speak of the harvest and of the notables of the village; his father had left Colleville and bought the farm of Les Ecots, so that now they would be neighbours. "Ah!" she exclaimed. He then added that his parents were looking around for a wife for him, but that he, himself, was not so anxious and preferred to wait for a girl who suited him. She hung her head. He then asked her whether she had ever thought of marrying. She replied, smilingly, that it was wrong of him to make fun of her. "Oh! no, I am in earnest," he said, and put his left arm around her waist while they sauntered along. The air was soft, the stars were bright, and the huge load of hay oscillated in front of them, drawn by four horses whose ponderous hoofs raised clouds of dust. Without a word from their driver they turned to the right. He kissed her again and she went home. The following week, Theodore obtained meetings.

They met in yards, behind walls or under isolated trees. She was not ignorant, as girls of well-to-do families are—for the animals had instructed her;—but her reason and her instinct of honour kept her from falling. Her resistance exasperated Theodore's love and so in order to satisfy it (or perchance ingenuously), he offered to marry her. She would not believe him at first, so he made solemn promises. But, in a short time he mentioned a difficulty; the previous year, his parents had purchased a substitute for him; but any day he might be drafted and the prospect of serving in the army alarmed him greatly. To Felicite his cowardice appeared a proof of his love for her, and her devotion to him grew stronger. When she met him, he would torture her with his fears and his entreaties. At last, he announced that he was going to the prefect himself for information, and would let her know everything on the following Sunday, between eleven o'clock and midnight.

When the time grew near, she ran to meet her lover.

But instead of Theodore, one of his friends was at the meeting-place.

He informed her that she would never see her sweetheart again; for, in order to escape the conscription, he had married a rich old woman, Madame Lehoussais, of Toucques.

The poor girl's sorrow was frightful. She threw herself on the ground, she cried and called on the Lord, and wandered around desolately until sunrise. Then she went back to the farm, declared her intention of leaving, and at the end of the month, after she had received her wages, she packed all her belongings in a handkerchief and started for Pont-l'Eveque.

In front of the inn, she met a woman wearing widow's weeds, and upon questioning her, learned that she was looking for a cook. The girl did not know very much, but appeared so willing and so modest in her requirements, that Madame Aubain finally said:

"Very well, I will give you a trial."

And half an hour later Felicite was installed in her house.

At first she lived in a constant anxiety that was caused by "the style of the household" and the memory of "Monsieur," that hovered over everything. Paul and Virginia, the one aged seven, and the other barely four, seemed made of some precious material; she carried them pig-a-back, and was greatly mortified when Madame Aubain forbade her to kiss them every other minute.

But in spite of all this, she was happy. The comfort of her new surroundings had obliterated her sadness.

Every Thursday, friends of Madame Aubain dropped in for a game of cards, and it was Felicite's duty to prepare the table and heat the foot-warmers. They arrived at exactly eight o'clock and departed before eleven.

Every Monday morning, the dealer in second-hand goods, who lived under the alley-way, spread out his wares on the sidewalk. Then the city would be filled with a buzzing of voices in which the neighing of horses, the bleating of lambs, the grunting of pigs, could be distinguished, mingled with the sharp sound of wheels on the cobble-stones. About twelve o'clock, when the market was in full swing, there appeared at the front door a tall, middle-aged peasant, with a hooked nose and a cap on the back of his head; it was Robelin, the farmer of Geffosses. Shortly afterwards came Liebard, the farmer of Toucques, short, rotund and ruddy, wearing a grey jacket and spurred boots.

Both men brought their landlady either chickens or cheese. Felicite would invariably thwart their ruses and they held her in great respect.

At various times, Madame Aubain received a visit from the Marquis de Gremanville, one of her uncles, who was ruined and lived at Falaise on the remainder of his estates. He always came at dinner-time and brought an ugly poodle with him, whose paws soiled their furniture. In spite of his efforts to appear a man of breeding (he even went so far as to raise his hat every time he said "My deceased father"), his habits got the better of him, and he would fill his glass a little too often and relate broad stories. Felicite would show him out very politely and say: "You have had enough for this time, Monsieur de Gremanville! Hoping to see you again!" and would close the door.

She opened it gladly for Monsieur Bourais, a retired lawyer. His bald head and white cravat, the ruffling of his shirt, his flowing brown coat, the manner in which he took snuff, his whole person, in fact, produced in her the kind of awe which we feel when we see extraordinary persons. As he managed Madame's estates, he spent hours with her in Monsieur's study; he was in constant fear of being compromised, had a great regard for the magistracy and some pretensions to learning.

In order to facilitate the children's studies, he presented them with an engraved geography which represented various scenes of the world; cannibals with feather head-dresses, a gorilla kidnapping a young girl, Arabs in the desert, a whale being harpooned, etc.

Paul explained the pictures to Felicite. And, in fact, this was her only literary education.

The children's studies were under the direction of a poor devil employed at the town-hall, who sharpened his pocket-knife on his boots and was famous for his penmanship.

When the weather was fine, they went to Geffosses. The house was built in the centre of the sloping yard; and the sea looked like a grey spot in the distance. Felicite would take slices of cold meat from the lunch basket and they would sit down and eat in a room next to the dairy. This room was all that remained of a cottage that had been torn down. The dilapidated wall-paper trembled in the drafts. Madame Aubain, overwhelmed by recollections, would hang her head, while the children were afraid to open their mouths. Then, "Why don't you go and play?" their mother would say; and they would scamper off.

Paul would go to the old barn, catch birds, throw stones into the pond, or pound the trunks of the trees with a stick till they resounded like drums. Virginia would feed the rabbits and run to pick the wild flowers in the fields, and her flying legs would disclose her little embroidered pantalettes. One autumn evening, they struck out for home through the meadows. The new moon illumined part of the sky and a mist hovered like a veil over the sinuosities of the river. Oxen, lying in the pastures, gazed mildly at the passing persons. In the third field, however, several of them got up and surrounded them. "Don't be afraid," cried Felicite; and murmuring a sort of lament she passed her hand over the back of the nearest ox; he turned away and the others followed. But when they came to the next pasture, they heard frightful bellowing.

It was a bull which was hidden from them by the fog. He advanced towards the two women, and Madame Aubain prepared to flee for her life. "No, no! not so fast," warned Felicite. Still they hurried on, for they could hear the noisy breathing of the bull behind them. His hoofs pounded the grass like hammers, and presently he began to gallop! Felicite turned around and threw patches of grass in his eyes. He hung his head, shook his horns and bellowed with fury. Madame Aubain and the children, huddled at the end of the field, were trying to jump over the ditch. Felicite continued to back before the bull, blinding him with dirt, while she shouted to them to make haste.

Madame Aubain finally slid into the ditch, after shoving first Virginia and then Paul into it, and though she stumbled several times she managed, by dint of courage, to climb the other side of it.

The bull had driven Felicite up against a fence; the foam from his muzzle flew in her face and in another minute he would have disembowelled her. She had just time to slip between two bars and the huge animal, thwarted, paused.

For years, this occurrence was a topic of conversation in Pont-l'Eveque. But Felicite took no credit to herself, and probably never knew that she had been heroic.

Virginia occupied her thoughts solely, for the shock she had sustained gave her a nervous affection, and the physician, M. Poupart, prescribed the salt-water bathing at Trouville. In those days, Trouville was not greatly patronised. Madame Aubain gathered information, consulted Bourais, and made preparations as if they were going on an extended trip.

The baggage was sent the day before on Liebard's cart. On the following morning, he brought around two horses, one of which had a woman's saddle with a velveteen back to it, while on the crupper of the other was a rolled shawl that was to be used for a seat. Madame Aubain mounted the second horse, behind Liebard. Felicite took charge of the little girl, and Paul rode M. Lechaptois' donkey, which had been lent for the occasion on the condition that they should be careful of it.

The road was so bad that it took two hours to cover the eight miles. The two horses sank knee-deep into the mud and stumbled into ditches; sometimes they had to jump over them. In certain places, Liebard's mare stopped abruptly. He waited patiently till she started again, and talked of the people whose estates bordered the road, adding his own moral reflections to the outline of their histories. Thus, when they were passing through Toucques, and came to some windows draped with nasturtiums, he shrugged his shoulders and said: "There's a woman, Madame Lehoussais, who, instead of taking a young man—" Felicite could not catch what followed; the horses began to trot, the donkey to gallop, and they turned into a lane; then a gate swung open, two farm-hands appeared and they all dismounted at the very threshold of the farm-house.

Mother Liebard, when she caught sight of her mistress, was lavish with joyful demonstrations. She got up a lunch which comprised a leg of mutton, tripe, sausages, a chicken fricassee, sweet cider, a fruit tart and some preserved prunes; then to all this the good woman added polite remarks about Madame, who appeared to be in better health, Mademoiselle, who had grown to be "superb," and Paul, who had become singularly sturdy; she spoke also of their deceased grandparents, whom the Liebards had known, for they had been in the service of the family for several generations.

Like its owners, the farm had an ancient appearance. The beams of the ceiling were mouldy, the walls black with smoke and the windows grey with dust. The oak sideboard was filled with all sorts of utensils, plates, pitchers, tin bowls, wolf-traps. The children laughed when they saw a huge syringe. There was not a tree in the yard that did not have mushrooms growing around its foot, or a bunch of mistletoe hanging in its branches. Several of the trees had been blown down, but they had started to grow in the middle and all were laden with quantities of apples. The thatched roofs, which were of unequal thickness, looked like brown velvet and could resist the fiercest gales. But the wagon-shed was fast crumbling to ruins. Madame Aubain said that she would attend to it, and then gave orders to have the horses saddled.

It took another thirty minutes to reach Trouville. The little caravan dismounted in order to pass Les Ecores, a cliff that overhangs the bay, and a few minutes later, at the end of the dock, they entered the yard of the Golden Lamb, an inn kept by Mother David.

During the first few days, Virginia felt stronger, owing to the change of air and the action of the sea-baths. She took them in her little chemise, as she had no bathing suit, and afterwards her nurse dressed her in the cabin of a customs officer, which was used for that purpose by other bathers.

In the afternoon, they would take the donkey and go to the Roches-Noires, near Hennequeville. The path led at first through undulating grounds, and thence to a plateau, where pastures and tilled fields alternated. At the edge of the road, mingling with the brambles, grew holly bushes, and here and there stood large dead trees whose branches traced zigzags upon the blue sky.

Ordinarily, they rested in a field facing the ocean, with Deauville on their left, and Havre on their right. The sea glittered brightly in the sun and was as smooth as a mirror, and so calm that they could scarcely distinguish its murmur; sparrows chirped joyfully and the immense canopy of heaven spread over it all. Madame Aubain brought out her sewing, and Virginia amused herself by braiding reeds; Felicite wove lavender blossoms, while Paul was bored and wished to go home.

Sometimes they crossed the Toucques in a boat, and started to hunt for sea-shells. The outgoing tide exposed star-fish and sea-urchins, and the children tried to catch the flakes of foam which the wind blew away. The sleepy waves lapping the sand unfurled themselves along the shore that extended as far as the eye could see, but where land began, it was limited by the downs which separated it from the "Swamp," a large meadow shaped like a hippodrome. When they went home that way, Trouville, on the slope of a hill below, grew larger and larger as they advanced, and, with all its houses of unequal height, seemed to spread out before them in a sort of giddy confusion.

When the heat was too oppressive, they remained in their rooms. The dazzling sunlight cast bars of light between the shutters. Not a sound in the village, not a soul on the sidewalk. This silence intensified the tranquility of everything. In the distance, the hammers of some calkers pounded the hull of a ship, and the sultry breeze brought them an odour of tar.

The principal diversion consisted in watching the return of the fishing-smacks. As soon as they passed the beacons, they began to ply to windward. The sails were lowered to one third of the masts, and with their fore-sails swelled up like balloons they glided over the waves and anchored in the middle of the harbour. Then they crept up alongside of the dock and the sailors threw the quivering fish over the side of the boat; a line of carts was waiting for them, and women with white caps sprang forward to receive the baskets and embrace their men-folk.

One day, one of them spoke to Felicite, who, after a little while, returned to the house gleefully. She had found one of her sisters, and presently Nastasie Barette, wife of Leroux, made her appearance, holding an infant in her arms, another child by the hand, while on her left was a little cabin-boy with his hands in his pockets and his cap on his ear.

At the end of fifteen minutes, Madame Aubain bade her go.

They always hung around the kitchen, or approached Felicite when she and the children were out walking. The husband, however, did not show himself.

Felicite developed a great fondness for them; she bought them a stove, some shirts and a blanket; it was evident that they exploited her. Her foolishness annoyed Madame Aubain, who, moreover did not like the nephew's familiarity, for he called her son "thou";—and, as Virginia began to cough and the season was over, she decided to return to Pont-l'Eveque.

Monsieur Bourais assisted her in the choice of a college. The one at Caen was considered the best. So Paul was sent away and bravely said good-bye to them all, for he was glad to go to live in a house where he would have boy companions.

Madame Aubain resigned herself to the separation from her son because it was unavoidable. Virginia brooded less and less over it. Felicite regretted the noise he made, but soon a new occupation diverted her mind; beginning from Christmas, she accompanied the little girl to her catechism lesson every day.

CHAPTER III

After she had made a curtsey at the threshold, she would walk up the aisle between the double lines of chairs, open Madame Aubain's pew, sit down and look around.

Girls and boys, the former on the right, the latter on the left-hand side of the church, filled the stalls of the choir; the priest stood beside the reading-desk; on one stained window of the side-aisle the Holy Ghost hovered over the Virgin; on another one, Mary knelt before the Child Jesus, and behind the altar, a wooden group represented Saint Michael felling the dragon.

The priest first read a condensed lesson of sacred history. Felicite evoked Paradise, the Flood, the Tower of Babel, the blazing cities, the dying nations, the shattered idols; and out of this she developed a great respect for the Almighty and a great fear of His wrath. Then, when she had listened to the Passion, she wept. Why had they crucified Him who loved little children, nourished the people, made the blind see, and who, out of humility, had wished to be born among the poor, in a stable? The sowings, the harvests, the wine-presses, all those familiar things which the Scriptures mention, formed a part of her life; the word of God sanctified them; and she loved the lambs with increased tenderness for the sake of the Lamb, and the doves because of the Holy Ghost.

She found it hard, however, to think of the latter as a person, for was it not a bird, a flame, and sometimes only a breath? Perhaps it is its light that at night hovers over swamps, its breath that propels the clouds, its voice that renders church-bells harmonious. And Felicite worshipped devoutly, while enjoying the coolness and the stillness of the church.

As for the dogma, she could not understand it and did not even try. The priest discoursed, the children recited, and she went to sleep, only to awaken with a start when they were leaving the church and their wooden shoes clattered on the stone pavement.

In this way, she learned her catechism, her religious education having been neglected in her youth; and thenceforth she imitated all Virginia's religious practices, fasted when she did, and went to confession with her. At the Corpus-Christi Day they both decorated an altar.

She worried in advance over Virginia's first communion. She fussed about the shoes, the rosary, the book and the gloves. With what nervousness she helped the mother dress the child!

During the entire ceremony, she felt anguished. Monsieur Bourais hid part of the choir from view, but directly in front of her, the flock of maidens, wearing white wreaths over their lowered veils, formed a snow-white field, and she recognised her darling by the slenderness of her neck and her devout attitude. The bell tinkled. All the heads bent and there was a silence. Then, at the peals of the organ the singers and the worshippers struck up the Agnes Dei; the boys' procession began; behind them came the girls. With clasped hands, they advanced step by step to the lighted altar, knelt at the first step, received one by one the Host, and returned to their seats in the same order. When Virginia's turn came, Felicite leaned forward to watch her, and through that imagination which springs from true affection, she at once became the child, whose face and dress became hers, whose heart beat in her bosom, and when Virginia opened her mouth and closed her lids, she did likewise and came very near fainting.

The following day, she presented herself early at the church so as to receive communion from the cure. She took it with the proper feeling, but did not experience the same delight as on the previous day.

Madame Aubain wished to make an accomplished girl of her daughter; and as Guyot could not teach English or music, she decided to send her to the Ursulines at Honfleur.

The child made no objection, but Felicite sighed and thought Madame was heartless. Then, she thought that perhaps her mistress was right, as these things were beyond her sphere. Finally, one day, an old fiacre stopped in front of the door and a nun stepped out. Felicite put Virginia's luggage on top of the carriage, gave the coachman some instructions, and smuggled six jars of jam, a dozen pears and a bunch of violets under the seat.

At the last minute, Virginia had a fit of sobbing; she embraced her mother again and again, while the latter kissed her on the forehead, and said: "Now, be brave, be brave!" The step was pulled up and the fiacre rumbled off.

Then Madame Aubain had a fainting spell, and that evening all her friends, including the two Lormeaus, Madame Lechaptois, the ladies Rochefeuille, Messieurs de Houppeville and Bourais, called on her and tendered their sympathy.

At first the separation proved very painful to her. But her daughter wrote her three times a week and the other days she, herself, wrote to Virginia. Then she walked in the garden, read a little, and in this way managed to fill out the emptiness of the hours.

Each morning, out of habit, Felicite entered Virginia's room and gazed at the walls. She missed combing her hair, lacing her shoes, tucking her in her bed, and the bright face and little hand when they used to go out for a walk. In order to occupy herself she tried to make lace. But her clumsy fingers broke the threads; she had no heart for anything, lost her sleep and "wasted away," as she put it.

In order to have some distraction, she asked leave to receive the visits of her nephew Victor.

He would come on Sunday, after church, with ruddy cheeks and bared chest, bringing with him the scent of the country. She would set the table and they would sit down opposite each other, and eat their dinner; she ate as little as possible, herself, to avoid any extra expense, but would stuff him so with food that he would finally go to sleep. At the first stroke of vespers, she would wake him up, brush his trousers, tie his cravat and walk to church with him, leaning on his arm with maternal pride.

His parents always told him to get something out of her, either a package of brown sugar, or soap, or brandy, and sometimes even money. He brought her his clothes to mend, and she accepted the task gladly, because it meant another visit from him.

In August, his father took him on a coasting-vessel.

It was vacation time and the arrival of the children consoled Felicite. But Paul was capricious, and Virginia was growing too old to be thee-and-thou'd, a fact which seemed to produce a sort of embarrassment in their relations.

Victor went successively to Morlaix, to Dunkirk, and to Brighton; whenever he returned from a trip he would bring her a present. The first time it was a box of shells; the second, a coffee-cup; the third, a big doll of ginger-bread. He was growing handsome, had a good figure, a tiny moustache, kind eyes, and a little leather cap that sat jauntily on the back of his head. He amused his aunt by telling her stories mingled with nautical expressions.

One Monday, the 14th of July, 1819 (she never forgot the date), Victor announced that he had been engaged on a merchant-vessel and that in two days he would take the steamer at Honfleur and join his sailer, which was going to start from Havre very soon. Perhaps he might be away two years.

The prospect of his departure filled Felicite with despair, and in order to bid him farewell, on Wednesday night, after Madame's dinner, she put on her pattens and trudged the four miles that separated Pont-l'Eveque from Honfleur.

When she reached the Calvary, instead of turning to the right, she turned to the left and lost herself in coal-yards; she had to retrace her steps; some people she spoke to advised her to hasten. She walked helplessly around the harbour filled with vessels, and knocked against hawsers. Presently the ground sloped abruptly, lights flitted to and fro, and she thought all at once that she had gone mad when she saw some horses in the sky.

Others, on the edge of the dock, neighed at the sight of the ocean. A derrick pulled them up in the air, and dumped them into a boat, where passengers were bustling about among barrels of cider, baskets of cheese and bags of meal; chickens cackled, the captain swore and a cabin-boy rested on the railing, apparently indifferent to his surroundings. Felicite, who did not recognise him, kept shouting: "Victor!" He suddenly raised his eyes, but while she was preparing to rush up to him, they withdrew the gangplank.

The packet, towed by singing women, glided out of the harbour. Her hull squeaked and the heavy waves beat up against her sides. The sail had turned and nobody was visible;—and on the ocean, silvered by the light of the moon, the vessel formed a black spot that grew dimmer and dimmer, and finally disappeared.

When Felicite passed the Calvary again, she felt as if she must entrust that which was dearest to her to the Lord; and for a long while she prayed, with uplifted eyes and a face wet with tears. The city was sleeping; some customs officials were taking the air; and the water kept pouring through the holes of the dam with a deafening roar. The town clock struck two.

The parlour of the convent would not open until morning, and surely a delay would annoy Madame, so, in spite of her desire to see the other child, she went home. The maids of the inn were just arising when she reached Pont-l'Eveque.

So the poor boy would be on the ocean for months! His previous trips had not alarmed her. One can come back from England and Brittany; but America, the colonies, the islands, were all lost in an uncertain region at the very end of the world.

From that time on, Felicite thought solely of her nephew. On warm days she feared he would suffer from thirst, and when it stormed, she was afraid he would be struck by lightning. When she harkened to the wind that rattled in the chimney and dislodged the tiles on the roof, she imagined that he was being buffeted by the same storm, perched on top of a shattered mast, with his whole body bend backward and covered with sea-foam; or,—these were recollections of the engraved geography—he was being devoured by savages, or captured in a forest by apes, or dying on some lonely coast. She never mentioned her anxieties, however.

Madame Aubain worried about her daughter.

The sisters thought that Virginia was affectionate but delicate. The slightest emotion enervated her. She had to give up her piano lessons. Her mother insisted upon regular letters from the convent. One morning, when thc postman failed to come, she grew impatient and began to pace to and fro, from her chair to the window. It was really extraordinary! No news since four days!

In order to console her mistress by her own example, Felicite said:

"Why, Madame, I haven't had any news since six months!—"

"From whom?—"

The servant replied gently:

"Why—from my nephew."

"Oh, yes, your nephew!" And shrugging her shoulders, Madame Aubain continued to pace the floor as if to say: "I did not think of it.—Besides, I do not care, a cabin-boy, a pauper!—but my daughter—what a difference! just think of it!—"

Felicite, although she had been reared roughly, was very indignant. Then she forgot about it.

It appeared quite natural to her that one should lose one's head about Virginia.

The two children were of equal importance; they were united in her heart and their fate was to be the same.

The chemist informed her that Victor's vessel had reached Havana. He had read the information in a newspaper.

Felicite imagined that Havana was a place where people did nothing but smoke, and that Victor walked around among negroes in a cloud of tobacco. Could a person, in case of need, return by land? How far was it from Pont-l'Eveque? In order to learn these things, she questioned Monsieur Bourais. He reached for his map and began some explanations concerning longitudes, and smiled with superiority at Felicite's bewilderment. At last, he took a pencil and pointed out an imperceptible black point in the scallops of an oval blotch, adding: "There it is." She bent over the map; the maze of coloured lines hurt her eyes without enlightening her; and when Bourais asked her what puzzled her, she requested him to show her the house Victor lived in. Bourais threw up his hands, sneezed, and then laughed uproariously; such ignorance delighted his soul; but Felicite failed to understand the cause of his mirth, she whose intelligence was so limited that she perhaps expected to see even the picture of her nephew!

It was two weeks later that Liebard came into the kitchen at market-time, and handed her a letter from her brother-in-law. As neither of them could read, she called upon her mistress.

Madame Aubain, who was counting the stitches of her knitting, laid her work down beside her, opened the letter, started, and in a low tone and with a searching look said: "They tell you of a—misfortune. Your nephew—"

He had died. The letter told nothing more.

Felicite dropped on a chair, leaned her head against the back, and closed her lids; presently they grew pink. Then, with drooping head, inert hands and staring eyes she repeated at intervals:

"Poor little chap! poor little chap!"

Liebard watched her and sighed. Madame Aubain was trembling.

She proposed to the girl to go to see her sister in Trouville.

With a single motion, Felicite replied that it was not necessary.

There was a silence. Old Liebard thought it about time for him to take leave.

Then Felicite uttered:

"They have no sympathy, they do not care!"

Her head fell forward again, and from time to time, mechanically, she toyed with the long knitting-needles on the work-table.

Some women passed through the yard with a basket of wet clothes.

When she saw them through the window, she suddenly remembered her own wash; as she had soaked it the day before, she must go and rinse it now. So she arose and left the room.

Her tub and her board were on the bank of the Toucques. She threw a heap of clothes on the ground, rolled up her sleeves and grasped her bat; and her loud pounding could be heard in the neighbouring gardens. The meadows were empty, the breeze wrinkled the stream, at the bottom of which were long grasses that looked like the hair of corpses floating in the water. She restrained her sorrow and was very brave until night; but, when she had gone to her own room, she gave way to it, burying her face in the pillow and pressing her two fists against her temples.

A long while afterward, she learned through Victor's captain, the circumstances which surrounded his death. At the hospital they had bled him too much, treating him for yellow fever. Four doctors held him at one time. He died almost instantly, and the chief surgeon had said:

"Here goes another one!"

His parents had always treated him barbarously; she preferred not to see them again, and they made no advances, either from forgetfulness or out of innate hardness.

Virginia was growing weaker.

A cough, continual fever, oppressive breathing and spots on her cheeks indicated some serious trouble. Monsieur Popart had advised a sojourn in Provence. Madame Aubain decided that they would go, and she would have had her daughter come home at once, had it not been for the climate of Pont-l'Eveque.

She made an arrangement with a livery-stable man who drove her over to the convent every Tuesday. In the garden there was a terrace, from which the view extends to the Seine. Virginia walked in it, leaning on her mother's arm and treading the dead vine leaves. Sometimes the sun, shining through the clouds, made her blink her lids, when she gazed at the sails in the distance, and let her eyes roam over the horizon from the chateau of Tancarville to the lighthouses of Havre. Then they rested on the arbour. Her mother had bought a little cask of fine Malaga wine, and Virginia, laughing at the idea of becoming intoxicated, would drink a few drops of it, but never more.

Her strength returned. Autumn passed. Felicite began to reassure Madame Aubain. But, one evening, when she returned home after an errand, she met M. Boupart's coach in front of the door; M. Boupart himself was standing in the vestibule and Madame Aubain was tying the strings of her bonnet. "Give me my foot-warmer, my purse and my gloves; and be quick about it," she said.

Virginia had congestion of the lungs; perhaps it was desperate.

"Not yet," said the physician, and both got into the carriage, while the snow fell in thick flakes. It was almost night and very cold.

Felicite rushed to the church to light a candle. Then she ran after the coach which she overtook after an hour's chase, sprang up behind and held on to the straps. But suddenly a thought crossed her mind: "The yard had been left open; supposing that burglars got in!" And down she jumped.

The next morning, at daybreak, she called at the doctor's. He had been home, but had left again. Then she waited at the inn, thinking that strangers might bring her a letter. At last, at daylight she took the diligence for Lisieux.

The convent was at the end of a steep and narrow street. When she arrived about at the middle of it, she heard strange noises, a funeral knell. "It must be for some one else," thought she; and she pulled the knocker violently.

After several minutes had elapsed, she heard footsteps, the door was half opened and a nun appeared. The good sister, with an air of compunction, told her that "she had just passed away." And at the same time the tolling of Saint-Leonard's increased.

Felicite reached the second floor. Already at the threshold, she caught sight of Virginia lying on her back, with clasped hands, her mouth open and her head thrown back, beneath a black crucifix inclined toward her, and stiff curtains which were less white than her face. Madame Aubain lay at the foot of the couch, clasping it with her arms and uttering groans of agony. The Mother Superior was standing on the right side of the bed. The three candles on the bureau made red blurs, and the windows were dimmed by the fog outside. The nuns carried Madame Aubain from the room.

For two nights, Felicite never left the corpse. She would repeat the same prayers, sprinkle holy water over the sheets, get up, come back to the bed and contemplate the body. At the end of the first vigil, she noticed that the face had taken on a yellow tinge, the lips grew blue, the nose grew pinched, the eyes were sunken. She kissed them several times and would not have been greatly astonished had Virginia opened them; to souls like this the supernatural is always quite simple. She washed her, wrapped her in a shroud, put her into the casket, laid a wreath of flowers on her head and arranged her curls. They were blond and of an extraordinary length for her age. Felicite cut off a big lock and put half of it into her bosom, resolving never to part with it.

The body was taken to Pont-l'Eveque, according to Madame Aubain's wishes; she followed the hearse in a closed carriage.

After the ceremony it took three quarters of an hour to reach the cemetery. Paul, sobbing, headed the procession; Monsieur Bourais followed, and then came the principal inhabitants of the town, the women covered with black capes, and Felicite. The memory of her nephew, and the thought that she had not been able to render him these honours, made her doubly unhappy, and she felt as if he were being buried with Virginia.

Madame Aubain's grief was uncontrollable. At first she rebelled against God, thinking that he was unjust to have taken away her child—she who had never done anything wrong, and whose conscience was so pure! But no! she ought to have taken her South. Other doctors would have saved her. She accused herself, prayed to be able to join her child, and cried in the midst of her dreams. Of the latter, one more especially haunted her. Her husband, dressed like a sailor, had come back from a long voyage, and with tears in his eyes told her that he had received the order to take Virginia away. Then they both consulted about a hiding-place.

Once she came in from the garden, all upset. A moment before (and she showed the place), the father and daughter had appeared to her, one after the other; they did nothing but look at her.

During several months she remained inert in her room. Felicite scolded her gently; she must keep up for her son and also for the other one, for "her memory."

"Her memory!" replied Madame Aubain, as if she were just awakening, "Oh! yes, yes, you do not forget her!" This was an allusion to the cemetery where she had been expressly forbidden to go.

But Felicite went there every day. At four o'clock exactly, she would go through the town, climb the hill, open the gate and arrive at Virginia's tomb. It was a small column of pink marble with a flat stone at its base, and it was surrounded by a little plot enclosed by chains. The flower-beds were bright with blossoms. Felicite watered their leaves, renewed the gravel, and knelt on the ground in order to till the earth properly. When Madame Aubain was able to visit the cemetery she felt very much relieved and consoled.

Years passed, all alike and marked by no other events than the return of the great church holidays: Easter, Assumption, All Saints' Day. Household happenings constituted the only data to which in later years they often referred. Thus, in 1825, workmen painted the vestibule; in 1827, a portion of the roof almost killed a man by falling into the yard. In the summer of 1828, it was Madame's turn to offer the hallowed bread; at that time, Bourais disappeared mysteriously; and the old acquaintances, Guyot, Liebard, Madame Lechaptois, Robelin, old Gremanville, paralysed since a long time, passed away one by one. One night, the driver of the mail in Pont-l'Eveque announced the Revolution of July. A few days afterward a new sub-prefect was nominated, the Baron de Larsonniere, ex-consul in America, who, besides his wife, had his sister-in-law and her three grown daughters with him. They were often seen on their lawn, dressed in loose blouses, and they had a parrot and a negro servant. Madame Aubain received a call, which she returned promptly. As soon as she caught sight of them, Felicite would run and notify her mistress. But only one thing was capable of arousing her: a letter from her son.

He could not follow any profession as he was absorbed in drinking. His mother paid his debts and he made fresh ones; and the sighs that she heaved while she knitted at the window reached the ears of Felicite who was spinning in the kitchen.

They walked in the garden together, always speaking of Virginia, and asking each other if such and such a thing would have pleased her, and what she would probably have said on this or that occasion.

All her little belongings were put away in a closet of the room which held the two little beds. But Madame Aubain looked them over as little as possible. One summer day, however, she resigned herself to the task and when she opened the closet the moths flew out.

Virginia's frocks were hung under a shelf where there were three dolls, some hoops, a doll-house, and a basic which she had used. Felicite and Madame Aubain also took out the skirts, the handkerchiefs, and the stockings and spread them on the beds, before putting them away again. The sun fell on the piteous things, disclosing their spots and the creases formed by the motions of the body. The atmosphere was warm and blue, and a blackbird trilled in the garden; everything seemed to live in happiness. They found a little hat of soft brown plush, but it was entirely moth-eaten. Felicite asked for it. Their eyes met and filled with tears; at last the mistress opened her arms and the servant threw herself against her breast and they hugged each other and giving vent to their grief in a kiss which equalised them for a moment.

It was the first time that this had ever happened, for Madame Aubain was not of an expansive nature. Felicite was as grateful for it as if it had been some favour, and thenceforth loved her with animal-like devotion and a religious veneration.

Her kind-heartedness developed. When she heard the drums of a marching regiment passing through the street, she would stand in the doorway with a jug of cider and give the soldiers a drink. She nursed cholera victims. She protected Polish refugees, and one of them even declared that he wished to marry her. But they quarrelled, for one morning when she returned from the Angelus she found him in the kitchen coolly eating a dish which he had prepared for himself during her absence.

After the Polish refugees, came Colmiche, an old man who was credited with having committed frightful misdeeds in '93. He lived near the river in the ruins of a pig-sty. The urchins peeped at him through the cracks in the walls and threw stones that fell on his miserable bed, where he lay gasping with catarrh, with long hair, inflamed eyelids, and a tumour as big as his head on one arm.

She got him some linen, tried to clean his hovel and dreamed of installing him in the bake-house without his being in Madame's way. When the cancer broke, she dressed it every day; sometimes she brought him some cake and placed him in the sun on a bundle of hay; and the poor old creature, trembling and drooling, would thank her in his broken voice, and put out his hands whenever she left him. Finally he died; and she had a mass said for the repose of his soul.

That day a great joy came to her: at dinner-time, Madame de Larsonniere's servant called with the parrot, the cage, and the perch and chain and lock. A note from the baroness told Madame Aubain that as her husband had been promoted to a prefecture, they were leaving that night, and she begged her to accept the bird as a remembrance and a token of her esteem.

Since a long time the parrot had been on Felicite's mind, because he came from America, which reminded her of Victor, and she had approached the negro on the subject.

Once even, she had said:

"How glad Madame would be to have him!"

The man had repeated this remark to his mistress who, not being able to keep the bird, took this means of getting rid of it.

CHAPTER IV

He was called Loulou. His body was green, his head blue, the tips of his wings were pink and his breast was golden.

But he had the tiresome tricks of biting his perch, pulling his feathers out, scattering refuse and spilling the water of his bath. Madame Aubain grew tired of him and gave him to Felicite for good.

She undertook his education, and soon he was able to repeat: "Pretty boy! Your servant, sir! I salute you, Marie!" His perch was placed near the door and several persons were astonished that he did not answer to the name of "Jacquot," for every parrot is called Jacquot. They called him a goose and a log, and these taunts were like so many dagger thrusts to Felicite. Strange stubbornness of the bird which would not talk when people watched him!

Nevertheless, he sought society; for on Sunday, when the ladies Rochefeuille, Monsieur de Houppeville and the new habitues, Onfroy, the chemist, Monsieur Varin and Captain Mathieu, dropped in for their game of cards, he struck the window-panes with his wings and made such a racket that it was impossible to talk.

Bourais' face must have appeared very funny to Loulou. As soon as he saw him he would begin to roar. His voice re-echoed in the yard, and the neighbours would come to the windows and begin to laugh, too; and in order that the parrot might not see him, Monsieur Bourais edged along the wall, pushed his hat over his eyes to hide his profile, and entered by the garden door, and the looks he gave the bird lacked affection. Loulou, having thrust his head into the butcher-boy's basket, received a slap, and from that time he always tried to nip his enemy. Fabu threatened to ring his neck, although he was not cruelly inclined, notwithstanding his big whiskers and tattooings. On the contrary, he rather liked the bird, and, out of devilry, tried to teach him oaths. Felicite, whom his manner alarmed, put Loulou in the kitchen, took off his chain and let him walk all over the house.

When he went downstairs, he rested his beak on the steps, lifted his right foot and then his left one; but his mistress feared that such feats would give him vertigo. He became ill and was unable to eat. There was a small growth under his tongue like those chickens are sometimes afflicted with. Felicite pulled it off with her nails and cured him. One day, Paul was imprudent enough to blow the smoke of his cigar in his face; another time, Madame Lormeau was teasing him with the tip of her umbrella and he swallowed the tip. Finally he got lost.

She had put him on the grass to cool him and went away only for a second; when she returned, she found no parrot! She hunted among the bushes, on the bank of the river, and on the roofs, without paying any attention to Madame Aubain who screamed at her: "Take care! you must be insane!" Then she searched every garden in Pont-l'Eveque and stopped the passers-by to inquire of them: "Haven't you perhaps seen my parrot?" To those who had never seen the parrot, she described him minutely. Suddenly she thought she saw something green fluttering behind the mills at the foot of the hill. But when she was at the top of the hill she could not see it. A hod-carrier told her that he had just seen the bird in Saint-Melaine, in Mother Simon's store. She rushed to the place. The people did not know what she was talking about. At last she came home, exhausted, with her slippers worn to shreds, and despair in her heart. She sat down on the bench near Madame and was telling of her search when presently a light weight dropped on her shoulder—Loulou! What the deuce had he been doing? Perhaps he had just taken a little walk around the town!

She did not easily forget her scare; in fact, she never got over it. In consequence of a cold, she caught a sore throat; and some time later she had an earache. Three years later she was stone deaf, and spoke in a very loud voice even in church. Although her sins might have been proclaimed throughout the diocese without any shame to herself, or ill effects to the community, the cure thought it advisable to receive her confession in the vestry-room.

Imaginary buzzings also added to her bewilderment. Her mistress often said to her: "My goodness, how stupid you are!" and she would answer: "Yes, Madame," and look for something.

The narrow circle of her ideas grew more restricted than it already was; the bellowing of the oxen, the chime of the bells no longer reached her intelligence. All things moved silently, like ghosts. Only one noise penetrated her ears; the parrot's voice.

As if to divert her mind, he reproduced for her the tick-tack of the spit in the kitchen, the shrill cry of the fish-vendors, the saw of the carpenter who had a shop opposite, and when the door-bell rang, he would imitate Madame Aubain: "Felicite! go to the front door."

They held conversations together, Loulou repeating the three phrases of his repertory over and over, Felicite replying by words that had no greater meaning, but in which she poured out her feelings. In her isolation, the parrot was almost a son, a love. He climbed upon her fingers, pecked at her lips, clung to her shawl, and when she rocked her head to and fro like a nurse, the big wings of her cap and the wings of the bird flapped in unison. When clouds gathered on the horizon and the thunder rumbled, Loulou would scream, perhaps because he remembered the storms in his native forests. The dripping of the rain would excite him to frenzy; he flapped around, struck the ceiling with his wings, upset everything, and would finally fly into the garden to play. Then he would come back into the room, light on one of the andirons, and hop around in order to get dry.

One morning during the terrible winter of 1837, when she had put him in front of the fire-place on account of the cold, she found him dead in his cage, hanging to the wire bars with his head down. He had probably died of congestion. But she believed that he had been poisoned, and although she had no proofs whatever, her suspicion rested on Fabu.

She wept so sorely that her mistress said: "Why don't you have him stuffed?"

She asked the advice of the chemist, who had always been kind to the bird.

He wrote to Havre for her. A certain man named Fellacher consented to do the work. But, as the diligence driver often lost parcels entrusted to him, Felicite resolved to take her pet to Honfleur herself.

Leafless apple-trees lined the edges of the road. The ditches were covered with ice. The dogs on the neighbouring farms barked; and Felicite, with her hands beneath her cape, her little black sabots and her basket, trotted along nimbly in the middle of the sidewalk. She crossed the forest, passed by the Haut-Chene, and reached Saint-Gatien.

Behind her, in a cloud of dust and impelled by the steep incline, a mail-coach drawn by galloping horses advanced like a whirlwind. When he saw a woman in the middle of the road, who did not get out of the way, the driver stood up in his seat and shouted to her and so did the postilion, while the four horses, which he could not hold back, accelerated their pace; the two leaders were almost upon her; with a jerk of the reins he threw them to one side, but, furious at the incident, he lifted his big whip and lashed her from her head to her feet with such violence that she fell to the ground unconscious.

Her first thought, when she recovered her senses, was to open the basket. Loulou was unharmed. She felt a sting on her right cheek; when she took her hand away it was red, for the blood was flowing.

She sat down on a pile of stones, and sopped her cheek with her handkerchief; then she ate a crust of bread she had put in her basket, and consoled herself by looking at the bird.

Arriving at the top of Ecquemanville, she saw the lights of Honfleur shining in the distance like so many stars; further on, the ocean spread out in a confused mass. Then a weakness came over her; the misery of her childhood, the disappointment of her first love, the departure of her nephew, the death of Virginia; all these things came back to her at once, and, rising like a swelling tide in her throat, almost choked her.

Then she wished to speak to the captain of the vessel, and without stating what she was sending, she gave him some instructions.

Fellacher kept the parrot a long time. He always promised that it would be ready for the following week; after six months he announced the shipment of a case, and that was the end of it. Really, it seemed as if Loulou would never come back to his home. "They have stolen him," thought Felicite.

Finally he arrived, sitting bold upright on a branch which could be screwed into a mahogany pedestal, with his foot in the air, his head on one side, and in his beak a nut which the naturalist, from love of the sumptuous, had gilded. She put him in her room.

This place, to which only a chosen few were admitted, looked like a chapel and a second-hand shop, so filled was it with devotional and heterogeneous things. The door could not be opened easily on account of the presence of a large wardrobe. Opposite the window that looked out into the garden, a bull's-eye opened on the yard; a table was placed by the cot and held a wash-basin, two combs, and a piece of blue soap in a broken saucer. On the walls were rosaries, medals, a number of Holy Virgins, and a holy-water basin made out of a cocoanut; on the bureau, which was covered with a napkin like an altar, stood the box of shells that Victor had given her; also a watering-can and a balloon, writing-books, the engraved geography and a pair of shoes; on the nail which held the mirror, hung Virginia's little plush hat! Felicite carried this sort of respect so far that she even kept one of Monsieur's old coats. All the things which Madame Aubain discarded, Felicite begged for her own room. Thus, she had artificial flowers on the edge of the bureau, and the picture of the Comte d'Artois in the recess of the window. By means of a board, Loulou was set on a portion of the chimney which advanced into the room. Every morning when she awoke, she saw him in the dim light of dawn and recalled bygone days and the smallest details of insignificant actions, without any sense of bitterness or grief.

As she was unable to communicate with people, she lived in a sort of somnambulistic torpor. The processions of Corpus-Christi Day seemed to wake her up. She visited the neighbours to beg for candlesticks and mats so as to adorn the temporary altars in the street.

In church, she always gazed at the Holy Ghost, and noticed that there was something about it that resembled a parrot. The likenesses appeared even more striking on a coloured picture by Espinal, representing the baptism of our Saviour. With his scarlet wings and emerald body, it was really the image of Loulou. Having bought the picture, she hung it near the one of the Comte d'Artois so that she could take them in at one glance.

They associated in her mind, the parrot becoming sanctified through the neighbourhood of the Holy Ghost, and the latter becoming more lifelike in her eyes, and more comprehensible. In all probability the Father had never chosen as messenger a dove, as the latter has no voice, but rather one of Loulou's ancestors. And Felicite said her prayers in front of the coloured picture, though from time to time she turned slightly towards the bird.

She desired very much to enter in the ranks of the "Daughters of the Virgin." But Madame Aubain dissuaded her from it.

A most important event occurred: Paul's marriage.

After being first a notary's clerk, then in business, then in the customs, and a tax collector, and having even applied for a position in the administration of woods and forests, he had at last, when he was thirty-six years old, by a divine inspiration, found his vocation: registrature! and he displayed such a high ability that an inspector had offered him his daughter and his influence.

Paul, who had become quite settled, brought his bride to visit his mother.

But she looked down upon the customs of Pont-l'Eveque, put on airs, and hurt Felicite's feelings. Madame Aubain felt relieved when she left.

The following week they learned of Monsieur Bourais' death in an inn. There were rumours of suicide, which were confirmed; doubts concerning his integrity arose. Madame Aubain looked over her accounts and soon discovered his numerous embezzlements; sales of wood which had been concealed from her, false receipts, etc. Furthermore, he had an illegitimate child, and entertained a friendship for "a person in Dozule."

These base actions affected her very much. In March, 1853, she developed a pain in her chest; her tongue looked as if it were coated with smoke, and the leeches they applied did not relieve her oppression; and on the ninth evening she died, being just seventy-two years old.

People thought that she was younger, because her hair, which she wore in bands framing her pale face, was brown. Few friends regretted her loss, for her manner was so haughty that she did not attract them. Felicite mourned for her as servants seldom mourn for their masters. The fact that

Madame should die before herself perplexed her mind and seemed contrary to the order of things, and absolutely monstrous and inadmissible. Ten days later (the time to journey from Besancon), the heirs arrived. Her daughter-in-law ransacked the drawers, kept some of the furniture, and sold the rest; then they went back to their own home.

Madame's armchair, foot-warmer, work-table, the eight chairs, everything was gone! The places occupied by the pictures formed yellow squares on the walls. They had taken the two little beds, and the wardrobe had been emptied of Virginia's belongings! Felicite went upstairs, overcome with grief.

The following day a sign was posted on the door; the chemist screamed in her ear that the house was for sale.

For a moment she tottered, and had to sit down.

What hurt her most was to give up her room,—so nice for poor Loulou! She looked at him in despair and implored the Holy Ghost, and it was this way that she contracted the idolatrous habit of saying her prayers kneeling in front of the bird. Sometimes the sun fell through the window on his glass eye, and lighted a spark in it which sent Felicite into ecstasy.

Her mistress had left her an income of three hundred and eighty francs. The garden supplied her with vegetables. As for clothes, she had enough to last her till the end of her days, and she economised on the light by going to bed at dusk.

She rarely went out, in order to avoid passing in front of the second-hand dealer's shop where there was some of the old furniture. Since her fainting spell, she dragged her leg, and as her strength was failing rapidly, old Mother Simon, who had lost her money in the grocery business, came very morning to chop the wood and pump the water.

Her eyesight grew dim. She did not open the shutters after that. Many years passed. But the house did not sell or rent. Fearing that she would be put out, Felicite did not ask for repairs. The laths of the roof were rotting away, and during one whole winter her bolster was wet. After Easter she spit blood.

Then Mother Simon went for a doctor. Felicite wished to know what her complaint was. But, being too deaf to hear, she caught only one word: "Pneumonia." She was familiar with it and gently answered:—"Ah! like Madame," thinking it quite natural that she should follow her mistress.

The time for the altars in the street drew near.

The first one was always erected at the foot of the hill, the second in front of the post-office, and the third in the middle of the street. This position occasioned some rivalry among the women and they finally decided upon Madame Aubain's yard.

Felicite's fever grew worse. She was sorry that she could not do anything for the altar. If she could, at least, have contributed something towards it! Then she thought of the parrot. Her neighbours objected that it would not be proper. But the cure gave his consent and she was so grateful for it that she begged him to accept after her death, her only treasure, Loulou. From Tuesday until Saturday, the day before the event, she coughed more frequently. In the evening her face was contracted, her lips stuck to her gums and she began to vomit; and on the following day, she felt so low that she called for a priest.

Three neighbours surrounded her when the dominie administered the Extreme Unction. Afterwards she said that she wished to speak to Fabu.

He arrived in his Sunday clothes, very ill at ease among the funereal surroundings.

"Forgive me," she said, making an effort to extend her arm, "I believed it was you who killed him!"

What did such accusations mean? Suspect a man like him of murder! And Fabu became excited and was about to make trouble.

"Don't you see she is not in her right mind?"

From time to time Felicite spoke to shadows. The women left her and Mother Simon sat down to breakfast.

A little later, she took Loulou and holding him up to Felicite:

"Say good-bye to him, now!" she commanded.

Although he was not a corpse, he was eaten up by worms; one of his wings was broken and the wadding was coming out of his body. But Felicite was blind now, and she took him and laid him against her cheek. Then Mother Simon removed him in order to set him on the altar.

CHAPTER V

The grass exhaled an odour of summer; flies buzzed in the air, the sun shone on the river and warmed the slated roof. Old Mother Simon had returned to Felicite and was peacefully falling asleep.

The ringing of bells woke her; the people were coming out of church. Felicite's delirium subsided. By thinking of the procession, she was able to see it as if she had taken part in it. All the school-children, the singers and the firemen walked on the sidewalks, while in the middle of the street came first the custodian of the church with his halberd, then the beadle with a large cross, the teacher in charge of the boys and a sister escorting the little girls; three of the smallest ones, with curly heads, threw rose leaves into the air; the deacon with outstretched arms conducted the music; and two incense-bearers turned with each step they took toward the Holy Sacrament, which was carried by M. le Cure, attired in his handsome chasuble and walking under a canopy of red velvet supported by four men. A crowd of people followed, jammed between the walls of the houses hung with white sheets; at last the procession arrived at the foot of the hill.

A cold sweat broke out on Felicite's forehead. Mother Simon wiped it away with a cloth, saying inwardly that some day she would have to go through the same thing herself.

The murmur of the crowd grew louder, was very distinct for a moment and then died away. A volley of musketry shook the window-panes. It was the postilions saluting the Sacrament. Felicite rolled her eyes, and said as loudly as she could:

"Is he all right?" meaning the parrot.

Her death agony began. A rattle that grew more and more rapid shook her body. Froth appeared at the corners of her mouth, and her whole frame trembled. In a little while could be heard the music of the bass horns, the clear voices of the children and the men's deeper notes. At intervals all was still, and their shoes sounded like a herd of cattle passing over the grass.

The clergy appeared in the yard. Mother Simon climbed on a chair to reach the bull's-eye, and in this manner could see the altar. It was covered with a lace cloth and draped with green wreaths. In the middle stood a little frame containing relics; at the corners were two little orange-trees, and all along the edge were silver candlesticks, porcelain vases containing sun-flowers, lilies, peonies, and tufts of hydrangeas. This mount of bright colours descended diagonally from the first floor to the carpet that covered the sidewalk. Rare objects arrested one's eye. A golden sugar-bowl was crowned with violets, earrings set with Alencon stones were displayed on green moss, and two Chinese screens with their bright landscapes were near by. Loulou, hidden beneath roses, showed nothing but his blue head which looked like a piece of lapis-lazuli.

The singers, the canopy-bearers and the children lined up against the sides of the yard. Slowly the priest ascended the steps and placed his shining sun on the lace cloth. Everybody knelt. There was deep silence; and the censers slipping on their chains were swung high in the air. A blue vapour rose in Felicite's room. She opened her nostrils and inhaled with a mystic sensuousness; then she closed her lids. Her lips smiled. The beats of her heart grew fainter and fainter, and vaguer, like a fountain giving out, like an echo dying away;—and when she exhaled her last breath, she thought she saw in the half-opened heavens a gigantic parrot hovering above her head.

Milton Keynes UK
Ingram Content Group UK Ltd.
UKHW010628080324
438959UK00005B/366